P9-DGI-723

The 500 Hats

OF BARTHOLOMEW CUBBINS

By Dr. Seuss

A Vanguard Press Book

RANDOM HOUSE NEW YORK

To
Chrysanthemum-Pearl

(aged 89 months, going on 90)

Library of Congress Cataloging-in-Publication Data:
Seuss, Dr.   The 500 Hats of Bartholomew Cubbins / by Dr. Seuss.   p.   cm.   "A Vanguard Press book."
SUMMARY: Each time Bartholomew Cubbins attempts to obey the King's order to take off his hat,
he finds there is another one on his head.
ISBN: 0-394-84484-X (trade) ; 0-394-94484-4 (lib. bdg.)
[1. Hats—Fiction.   2. Fairy tales]   I. Title.   II. Title: Five hundred hats of Bartholomew Cubbins.
PZ8.G326Fi   1989   [E]—dc19   88-38412

Manufactured in the United States of America

25 26 27 28 29 30

IN THE beginning, Bartholomew Cubbins didn't have five hundred hats. He had only one hat. It was an old one that had belonged to his father and his father's father before him. It was probably the oldest and the plainest hat in the whole Kingdom of Didd, where Bartholomew Cubbins lived. But Bartholomew liked it—especially because of the feather that always pointed straight up in the air.

The Kingdom of Didd was ruled by King Derwin. His palace stood high on the top of the mountain. From his balcony, he looked down over the houses of all his subjects—first, over the spires of the noblemen's castles, across the broad roofs of the rich men's mansions, then over the little houses of the townsfolk, to the huts of the farmers far off in the fields.

It was a mighty view and it made King Derwin feel mighty important.

Far off in the fields, on the edge of a cranberry bog, stood the hut of the Cubbins family. From the small door Bartholomew looked across the huts of the farmers to the houses of the townsfolk, then to the rich men's mansions and the noblemen's castles, up to the great towering palace of the King. It was exactly the same view that King Derwin saw from his balcony, but Bartholomew saw it backward.

It was a mighty view, but it made Bartholomew Cubbins feel mighty small.

Just after sunrise one Saturday morning Bartholomew started for town. He felt very happy. A pleasant breeze whistled through the feather in his hat. In his right hand he carried a basket of cranberries to sell at the market. He was anxious to sell them quickly and bring the money back home to his parents.

He walked faster and faster till he got to the gates of the town.

The sound of silver trumpets rang through the air. Hoof beats clattered on the cobbled streets.

"Clear the way! Clear the way! Make way for the King!"

All the people rushed for the sidewalks. They drove their carts right up over the curbstones. Bartholomew clutched his basket tighter.

Around the corner dashed fifty trumpeters on yellow-robed horses. Behind them on crimson-robed horses came the King's Own Guards.

"Hats off to the King!" shouted the Captain of the King's Own Guards.

On came the King's carriage — white and gold and purple. It rumbled like thunder through the narrow street.

It swept past Bartholomew. Then suddenly its mighty brakes shrieked. It lurched—and then it stopped. The whole procession stood still.

Bartholomew could hardly believe what he saw. Through the side window of the carriage, the King himself was staring back—straight back at him! Bartholomew began to tremble.

"Back up!" the King commanded the Royal Coachman.

The Royal Coachman shouted to the royal horses. The King's Own Guards shouted to their crimson-robed horses. The trumpeters shouted to their yellow-robed horses. Very slowly the whole procession backed down the street, until the King's carriage stopped right in front of Bartholomew.

The King leaned from his carriage window and fixed his eyes directly on Bartholomew Cubbins. "Well...? Well...?" he demanded.

Bartholomew shook with fright. "I ought to say something," he thought to himself. But he could think of nothing to say.

"Well?" demanded the King again. "Do you or do you *not* take off your hat before your King?"

"Yes, indeed, Sire," answered Bartholomew, feeling greatly relieved. "I *do* take off my hat before my King."

"Then take it off this very instant," commanded the King more loudly than before.

"But, Sire, my hat *is* off," answered Bartholomew.

"Such impudence!" shouted the King, shaking an angry finger. "How dare you stand there and tell me your hat is off!"

"I don't like to say you are wrong, Sire," said Bartholomew very politely, "but you see my hat *is* off." And he showed the King the hat in his hand.

"If that's your hat in your hand," demanded the King, "what's that on your head?"

"On my head?" gasped Bartholomew. There *did* seem to be something on his head. He reached up his hand and touched a hat!

The face of Bartholomew Cubbins turned very red. "It's a hat, Sire," he stammered, "but it *can't* be mine. Someone behind me must have put it on my head."

"I don't care *how* it got there," said the King. "You take it off." And the King sat back in his carriage.

Bartholomew quickly snatched off the hat. He stared at it in astonishment. It was exactly the same as his own hat—the same size, the same color. And it had exactly the same feather.

"By the Crown of my Fathers!" roared the King, again leaning out of the carriage window. "Did I or did I *not* command you to take off your hat?"

"You did, Sire. . . . I took it off . . . I took it off twice."

"Nonsense! There is still a hat upon your head."

"Another hat?" Again Bartholomew reached up his hand and touched a hat.

"Come, come, what is the meaning of all this?" demanded the King, his face purple with rage.

"I don't know, Sire," answered Bartholomew. "It never happened to me before."

The King was now shaking with such fury that the carriage rocked on its wheels and the Royal Coachman could hardly sit in his seat. "Arrest this impudent trickster," shouted the King to the Captain of the King's Own Guards. "We'll teach him to take off his hat."

The Royal Coachman cracked his long whip. The King's carriage swung forward up the street toward the palace.

But the Captain of the King's Own Guards leaned down from his big brass saddle and grabbed Bartholomew Cubbins by his shirt. Away flew Bartholomew's basket! The cranberries bounced over the cobblestones and rolled down into the gutter.

With a jangling of spurs and a clatter of horseshoes, the Captain and Bartholomew sped up the winding street toward the palace. Out of the narrow streets, on up the hill! Bartholomew clung to the Captain's broad back. On and on they galloped, past the bright gardens of the wealthy merchants. Higher and higher up the mountain, on past the walls of the noblemen's castles. . . .

Flupp! . . . the sharp wind whisked off Bartholomew's hat. *Flupp Flupp* . . . two more flew off. *Flupp Flupp Flupp* flew another . . . and another. ". . . 4 . . . 5 . . . 6 . . . 7 . . ." Bartholomew kept counting as the hats came faster and faster. Lords and ladies stared from the windows of their turrets, wondering what the strange stream of hats could mean.

Over the palace drawbridge they sped—through the great gates, and into the courtyard. The Captain pulled in his reins.

"His Majesty waits in the Throne Room," said a guard, saluting the Captain.

"The Throne Room!" The Captain dropped Bartholomew to the ground. "I'd certainly hate to be in your shoes," he said, shaking his head sadly.

For a moment Bartholomew was terribly frightened. "Still," he thought to himself, "the King can do nothing dreadful to punish me, because I really haven't done anything wrong. It would be cowardly to feel afraid."

Bartholomew threw back his shoulders and marched straight ahead into the palace. "Follow the black carpet," said the guard at the door. All through the long hallway Bartholomew could hear the muttering of voices behind heavy doors. "He won't take off his hat?" "No, he won't take off his hat."

Bartholomew walked on till he stood
in the very middle of the Throne Room.
The King, in a long scarlet robe, was sitting on
his throne. Beside him stood Sir Alaric, Keeper of
the King's Records. He wore in his belt, instead of a
sword, a long silver ruler. Lords and noblemen of the
court stood solemn and silent.

The King looked down at Bartholomew severely. "Young man,
I'll give you one more chance. Will you take off your hat for your
King?"

"Your Majesty," said Bartholomew as politely as he possibly could,
"I will—but I'm afraid it won't do any good." And he took off his hat—
and it didn't do any good. Another hat sat on Bartholomew's head.
He took off hat after hat after hat after hat until he was standing in the
middle of a great pile of hats.

The lords and noblemen were so astonished they couldn't even
speak. Such a thing had never happened in the Throne Room before.

"Heavens!" said Sir Alaric, Keeper of the Records, blinking behind his triangular spectacles. "He's taken off 45!"

"And there were 3 more down in the town," said the King.

"And you must add on 87 more that blew off my head as we galloped up the hill," said Bartholomew, trying to be helpful.

"One hundred and thirty-five hats! Most unusual," said Sir Alaric, writing it down on a long scroll.

"Come, come," said the King impatiently. "Sir Alaric, what do you make of all this nonsense?"

"Very *serious* nonsense, Your Majesty," answered Sir Alaric. "I advise you to call in an expert on hats."

"Excellent," agreed the King. "Ho, Guard! Fetch in Sir Snipps, maker of hats for all the fine lords."

Into the Throne Room marched the smallest man, wearing the tallest hat that Bartholomew had ever seen. It was Sir Snipps. Instead of a sword, he wore at his side a large pair of scissors.

"Take a look at this boy's hat," commanded the King. Sir Snipps looked at Bartholomew Cubbins' hat and sniffed in disgust. Then he turned to the King and bowed stiffly. "Your Majesty, I, Sir Snipps, am the maker of hats for all the fine lords. I make hats of cloth of gold, fine silks and gems and ostrich plumes. You ask *me* what *I* think of *this* hat? Pooh! It is the most ordinary hat I ever set eyes on."

"In that case," said the King, "it should be very simple for you to take it off."

"Simple, indeed," mumbled Sir Snipps haughtily, and, standing on his tiptoes, he pushed his pudgy thumb at Bartholomew's hat and knocked it to the floor. Immediately another appeared on Bartholomew's head.

"Screebees!" screamed Sir Snipps, leaping in the air higher than he was tall. Then he turned and ran shrieking out of the Throne Room.

"Dear me!" said the King, looking very puzzled. "If Snipps can't do it, this *must* be more than an ordinary hat."

"One hundred and thirty-six," wrote Sir Alaric, wrinkling his brow. "Your Majesty, I advise that you call in your Wise Men."

"A fine idea!" said the King. "Ho, Guard! bring me Nadd. Nadd knows about everything in all my kingdom."

In came an old, old man. He looked at the hat on Bartholomew's head, and he looked at the pile of hats on the floor.

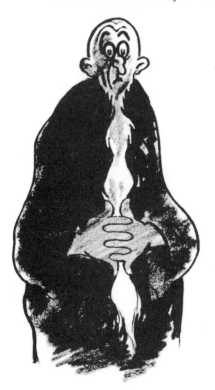

"Nadd, my Wise Man, can you take off his hat?" asked the King. Nadd shook his head solemnly—solemnly no.

"Then fetch me the Father of Nadd," commanded the King. "He knows about everything in all my kingdom and in all the world beyond."

In came an even older man. But when he looked at Bartholomew's hats, the Father of Nadd merely locked his fingers across his beard and said nothing.

"Then bring me the Father of
the Father of Nadd!" ordered the
King. "He knows about everything in all my kingdom, in all the
world beyond, and in all other worlds that may happen to be."

Then came the oldest man of them all. But he just looked at Bartholomew and nibbled nervously at the end of his beard.

"Does this mean there is *no one* in my whole kingdom who can take
off this boy's hat?" bellowed the King in a terrifying voice.

A small voice came up through the balcony window. "What's
the matter, Uncle Derwin?" To Bartholomew, it sounded like the
voice of a boy.

The King stepped out on the balcony and leaned over the marble
railing. "There's a boy in here . . . just about your age," the King said.
"He won't take off his hat."

Bartholomew tiptoed up behind the King and looked down. There stood a boy with a big lace collar—a very proud little boy with his nose in the air. It was the Grand Duke Wilfred, nephew of the King.

"You send him down here," said the Grand Duke Wilfred. *"I'll fix him."*

The King thought for a minute. He pushed back his crown and scratched his head. "Well...maybe you can. There's no harm trying."

"Take him to the Grand Duke Wilfred!" commanded the King. And two of the King's Own Guards led Bartholomew out of the Throne Room.

"Pooh!" said the Grand Duke Wilfred, looking at Bartholomew's hat and laughing meanly. "*That* hat won't come off? You stand over there." He pointed to a corner where the wall curved out. "I need a little target practise with my bow and arrow."

When Bartholomew saw that the Grand Duke Wilfred had only a child's bow he didn't feel frightened. He spoke up proudly, "*I* can shoot with my father's big bow."

"My bow's plenty big enough for shooting hats—especially hats like yours," answered Wilfred. And he let fly an arrow. zzZ! . . . it grazed Bartholomew's forehead and nipped off his hat. Away it blew, and over the parapet. But another hat appeared on his head. zzZ! . . . zzZ! . . . zzZ! . . . the arrows flew . . . till the Grand Duke's whole bagful of arrows was gone. And still a hat sat upon Bartholomew's head.

"It's not fair," cried the Grand Duke. "It's not fair!" He threw down his bow and stamped upon it.

"One hundred and fifty-four hats!" gulped Sir Alaric.

"These hats are driving me mad!" The King's voice rang out through all the palace. "Why waste time with a *child's* bow and arrow. Fetch me the mightiest bow and arrow in all my realm—fetch the Yeoman of the Bowmen!"

"Yeoman of the Bowmen," echoed all the lords and noblemen of the court.

A gigantic man strode out across the terrace. His bow was as big as the branch of a tree. The arrow was twice as long as Bartholomew, and thicker than his wrist.

"Yeoman of the Bowmen," said the King, "shoot off this boy's hat . . . and make it *stay* off!"

Bartholomew was trembling so hard that he could scarcely stand straight. The Yeoman bent back his mighty bow.

G—r—r—zibb! . . . Like a mad giant hornet the arrow tore through the air toward Bartholomew Cubbins.

G—r—r—zapp! . . . The sharp arrow head bit through his hat and carried it off—on and on for a full half mile.

G—r—r—zopp! . . . It plunked to a stop in the heart of an oak tree. Yet there on Bartholomew's head sat another hat.

The face of the Yeoman of the Bowmen went white as the palace walls. "It's black magic!" he shrieked.

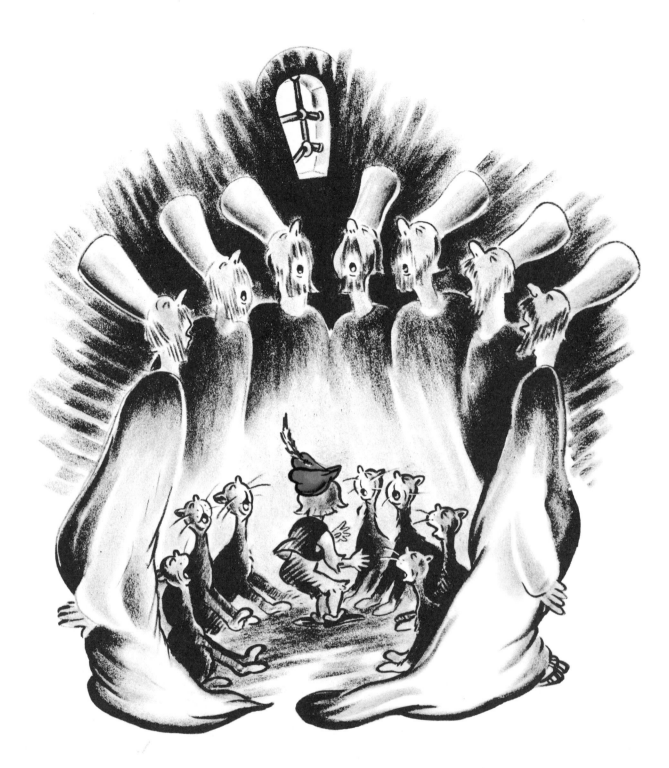

"Black magic, that's *just* what it is," sighed the King with relief. "I should have thought of that before. That makes things simple. Back to the Throne Room! Call my magicians!"

In the whole Throne Room there wasn't a sound as loud as a breath. But from the spiral stairs that led down from the southwest tower came the shuffling of slow, padded feet. The magicians were coming! Low and slow, they were chanting words that were strange . . .

"Dig a hole five furlongs deep,
Down to where the night snakes creep,
Mix and mold the mystic mud,
Malber, Balber, Tidder, Tudd."

In came seven black-gowned magicians, and beside each one stalked a lean black cat. They circled around Bartholomew Cubbins muttering deep and mysterious sounds.

"Stop this useless muttering," ordered the King. "I want a chant that will charm away this boy's hat."

The magicians huddled over Bartholomew and chanted.

"Winkibus
Tinkibus
Fotichee
Klay,
Hat on this demon's head,
Fly far away!
Howl, men, howl away,
Howl away, howl away,
Yowl, cats, yowl away,
Yowl away, yowl away!
Hat on this demon's head,
Seep away, creep away, leap away, gleap away,
Never come back!"

"A mighty good chant," said the King, looking very pleased. "Are you sure it will work?"

All the magicians nodded together.

"But," said the King, looking puzzled, "there still *seems* to be a hat upon his head. How long will it take for the charm to work?"

"Be calm, oh, Sire, and have no fears," chanted the magicians.

"Our charm will work in ten short years."

"Ten years!" gasped the King. "Away, fools!" he shouted. "Out of my sight! I can't wait *ten years* to get rid of his hat. Oh, dear, what *can* I do . . . what CAN I do?"

"If I were King," whispered the Grand Duke Wilfred, "I'd chop off his head."

"A dreadful thought," said the King, biting his lip. "But I'm afraid I'll have to."

"Young man," he said to Bartholomew Cubbins, and he pointed to a small door at the end of the room, "march down those steps to the dungeon and tell the executioner to chop off your head."

Bartholomew's heart sank into his boots, but he did as the King commanded. "I *must* take off my hat," he said to himself as he started down the long black stairway. "This is my last chance." One

hat after another he tore from his head "...156...157...158..." It grew colder and damper. "...217...218...219..." Down... down...down. "...231...232...233..." It seemed to Bartholomew he must be in the very heart of the mountain.

"Who's there?" said a voice from the blackness.

Bartholomew turned a corner and stepped into the dungeon.

The executioner was whistling and swinging his axe idly, because at the moment he had nothing to do. In spite of his business, he really seemed to be a very pleasant man.

"The King says you must chop off my head," said Bartholomew.

"Oh, I'd hate to," said the executioner, looking at him with a friendly smile. "You seem like such a nice boy."

"Well . . . the King says you have to," said Bartholomew, "so please get it over with."

"All right," sighed the executioner, "but first you've got to take off your hat."

"Why?" asked Bartholomew.

"I don't know," said the executioner, "but it's one of the rules. I can't execute anyone with his hat on."

"All right," said Bartholomew, "you take it off for me."

The executioner leaned across the chopping block and flipped off Bartholomew's hat.

"What's this?" he gasped, blinking through the holes in his mask, as another hat sat on Bartholomew's head. He flipped this one off . . . then another and another.

"Fiddlesticks!" grunted the executioner, throwing his axe on the floor. "I can't execute you at all." And he shook hands with Bartholo- mew and sent him back upstairs to the King.

The King had been taking a nap on the throne. "What are you doing back here?" he said to Bartholomew, angry at being awakened.

"I'm sorry, Your Majesty," explained Bartholomew. "My head can't come off with my hat on. . . . It's against the rules."

"So it can't," said the King, leaning back wearily. "Now how many hats does that make altogether?"

"The executioner knocked off 13 . . . and I left 178 more on the dungeon steps," answered Bartholomew.

"Three hundred and forty-six hats," mumbled Sir Alaric from behind his scroll.

"Uncle Derwin," yawned the Grand Duke Wilfred, "I suppose I'll have to do away with him. Send him up to the highest turret and I, in person, will push him off."

"Wilfred! I'm surprised at you," said the King. "But I guess it's a good idea."

So the King and the Grand Duke led Bartholomew Cubbins toward the highest turret.

Up and up and up the turret stairs he climbed behind them.

"This is my *last*—my *very last* chance," thought Bartholomew. He snatched off his hat. "Three hundred and forty-seven!" He snatched off another. He pulled and he tore and he flung them behind him. ". . . 398 . . 399 . . ." His arms ached from pulling off hats. But still the hats came. Bartholomew climbed on.

". . . 448 . . . 449 . . . 450 . . ." counted Sir Alaric, puffing up the stairs behind him.

Suddenly Sir Alaric stopped. He looked. He took off his triangular spectacles and wiped them on his sleeve. And then he looked again. *The hats began to change!* Hat 451 had, not one, but *two* feathers! Hat 452 had three . . . and 453 also had three *and a little red jewel!* Each new hat was fancier than the hat just before.

"Your Majesty! Your Majesty!" cried out Sir Alaric.

But the King and the Grand Duke were 'way up where they couldn't hear. They had already reached the top of the highest turret. Bartholomew was following just behind.

"Step right out here and get out on that wall," snapped the Grand Duke Wilfred. "I can't wait to push you off."

But when Bartholomew stepped up on the wall they gasped in amazement. He was wearing the most beautiful hat that had ever been seen in the Kingdom of Didd. It had a ruby larger than any the King himself had ever owned. It had ostrich plumes, and cockatoo plumes, and mockingbird plumes, and paradise plumes. Beside *such* a hat even the King's Crown seemed like nothing.

The Grand Duke Wilfred took a quick step forward. Bartholomew thought his end had come at last.

"Wait!" shouted the King. He could not take his eyes off the magnificent hat.

"I *won't* wait," the Grand Duke talked back to the King. "I'm going to push him off now! That new big hat makes me madder than ever." And he flung out his arms to push Bartholomew off.

But the King was quicker than Wilfred. He grabbed him by the back of his fine lace collar. "This is to teach you," His Majesty said sternly, "that Grand Dukes *never* talk back to their King." And he turned the Grand Duke Wilfred over his knee and spanked him soundly, right on the seat of his royal silk pants.

"And now," smiled the King, lifting Bartholomew down from the wall, "it would be nice if you'd sell me that wonderful hat!"

". . . 498 . . . 499 . . ." broke in the tired voice of Sir Alaric, who had just arrived at the top of the steps, "and *that* . . ." he pointed to the hat on Bartholomew's head, "makes exactly 500!"

"Five Hundred!" exclaimed the King. "Will you sell it for 500 pieces of gold?"

"Anything you say, Sire," answered Bartholomew. "You see . . . I've never sold one before."

The King's hands trembled with joy as he reached for the hat.

Slowly, slowly, Bartholomew felt the weight of the great hat lifting from his head. He held his breath. . . . Then suddenly he felt the cool evening breezes blow through his hair. His face broke into a happy smile. The head of Bartholomew Cubbins was bare!

"Look, Your Majesty! *Look!*" he shouted to the King.

"No! *You* look at *me,*" answered the King. And he put the great hat on right over his crown.

Arm in arm, the King and Bartholomew went down to the counting room to count out the gold. Then the King sent Bartholomew home to his parents . . . no basket on his arm, no hat on his head, but with five hundred pieces of gold in a bag.

And the King commanded that the hat he had bought, and all the other hats, too, be kept forever in a great crystal case by the side of his throne.

But neither Bartholomew Cubbins, nor King Derwin himself, nor anyone else in the Kingdom of Didd could ever explain how the strange thing had happened. They only could say it just "happened to happen" and was not very likely to happen again.